THE TOWN HALL CLOCK

There was something different about the village of Hatsoff this bright Autumnal morning. People would walk out of their homes or step out of their business's and stand in the centre looking around and then go back inside to continue whatever it was that they had been doing.

Later they would step outside once again and look up and down the street, peer at each other then shrug their shoulders and go back inside again.

Bob Bowler would come out of his bank, Bertha Bonnet came out of her Florists and Billy Boater the general store owner, all stood looking at each other thinking that something was not quite right but not knowing what it could be, so back they went inside and carried on as usual.

It was Bobby Helmet the Chief of Police who solved the mystery. He arrived in the middle of the village as he often did to buy his morning newspaper, The Daily Topper, and stopped to check his police watch with the Town Hall Clock as he did every morning, when he noticed that the Great Town Hall Clock has stopped. 'My word' he said, 'the Town Hall clock has stopped at Eight Fifteen and it is now almost Nine

O'clock. 'What ever is going on'?

Just then the rest of the villagers sensed that the mystery may have been solved and out they all came to stand and stare at the non-moving Town Hall clock. 'I'd best get Tommy Trilby down here to investigate why the Town Hall clock has stopped' said Bobby, and the others nodded in agreement. 'Trilby, Detective will get to the bottom of this'.

With the Town Hall clock not working there had been no bell sounding every fifteen minutes and that is what had thrown the good people of Hatsoff into confusion. They were so used to hearing the bell chime that when it didn't they missed it but were unable to decide what it was that they were missing.

Trilby, Detective, arrived within minutes, not that anybody noticed as the clock had stopped and minutes meant nothing. 'Sort this problem out Tommy' said Bobby Helmet, 'I must go and buy my newspaper before they are all sold out'. So Trilby started by asking the villagers when they had first noticed that they bell was not chiming. Unfortunately nobody could answer his question as they did not realise that it was the bell chiming every fifteen minutes that they were missing and therefore could not tell him when they had first noticed it that wasn't working as they didn't know until The Police Chief told them. 'Or something like that' they all agreed. 'I had better go inside the Town Hall and investigate further' thought Tommy and off he went.

Bob Bowler the bank manager went with Tommy as he was the Lord Mayor of

Hatsoff and thought that it is only right that he should be part of the investigation. Bob showed Tommy to the door that lead to the clock tower and up they climbed the many stairs until they reached the top of the Tower and saw all the cogs and wheels and the great bell that made up the workings of the Town Hall clock.

Tommy looked out of the side of the Tower, 'you can see my house from here' he said to The Mayor. 'Yes, it is a lovely view from this high up Tommy but what about the clock'? 'Oh yes', said Tommy, 'I will continue to investigate this mystery'.

Tommy looked up in the rafters and down to the bottom of the Tower which made him quite dizzy. He checked the levers and the settings but still nothing.

Then he heard a quiet cheeping of bird noise that seemed to be coming from the very workings of the clocks huge wheels and cogs. He leaned into the inside of the clock and there saw a nest of young birds settled in their beds chirping away as if waiting for their breakfast. Tommy then noticed the Mother bird perched high in the roof watching every move that Tommy made. 'Don't worry', he said to the bird, 'I am only here to help get the clock working.

Then Tommy noticed that the nest was built into the cogs that played the Hatsoff Anthem, *'Hats Off to Hatsoff'*, at Nine O'clock on the first day of every new month and as it was the first day of a new month today the great cogs would start to turn soon to play their monthly tune. This would be a disaster for the nest and the little birds that sat in it happily tweeting away.

'I must try to get the nest out of danger', said Tommy, 'but why has the clock stopped'? The answer came when he looked outside at the great fingers of the clock and saw Ginger, one of Bertha Bonnets rather overweight cats sitting on the hour hand unable to move in or out without falling. 'Hello Ginger', said Tommy, 'I guess that you thought that you could chase these little birds but you did not expect to be stuck out there on the hour hand, no wonder the clock has stopped. Your little escapade to catch the birds may well have saved them from being crushed by the clocks great cogs'.

'Well, first things first' said Detective Trilby, 'I must secure the safety of the little birds in the nest and then get to you somehow Ginger'. So, in Tommy went and after asking the Mayor to contact the Fire Brigade, he went back to the great clock to try to get the nest to a safe place. It was not going to be easy. The nest was stuck fast into the cogs thanks to the birds proud parent's making such a fine nest for their young. Tommy could not quite reach the nest so had to come up with another way to move the birds to safety. He went back down to street level and went into Bertha

Bonnet's hat shop and explained the situation. As it was one of Bertha's cats that were the cause of the problem, she was only too pleased to help. Tommy asked Bertha for two of the largest hat pins that she had in the shop. He then fastened both pins to Bertha's walking cane with sticky tape and set off back up to the Tower.

As Tommy reached the top he heard the Fire Engine arrive in front of the Town Hall and new that The Fire Chief, Henry Hardhat would take control of rescuing Ginger from the Hour hand. Tommy then went about his business of saving the birds in the nest whilst Henry rescued the cat. Tommy reached into the cogs and wheels with the walking cane and the two huge hat pins. He slid the pins into either side of the nest making sure not to disturb the young chicks and had the idea of lifting the nest to safety in one smooth sweep.

Unfortunately, just as Tommy was about to raise

the nest, Henry Hardhats extending ladder reached the clock face to rescue Ginger. The cat got such a fright at seeing Henry rise towards him that he summoned the courage for one great leap from the Hour hand, into the clock tower, onto the Great Bell and then away down the stairs into the safety of

Bertha's Hat Shop and once there he curled up in one of Bertha's old hat boxes that he used as a bed and as if nothing had happened he went fast to sleep.

The rather large cat leaving the Hour Hand and landing on the Great Bell set the whole system into automatic reset mode. This meant that the clock reset itself for time and the Great Bell started chiming and the Monthly Anthem cogs started turning. The nest was now moving along into the turning cogs and wheels and was in great danger of being crushed flat. The Fire Chief, Henry Hardhat, had been told of the situation facing the young birds by The Mayor and so instantly he leapt from the ladder and grabbed hold of the Hour Hand to stop it from reaching Nine O'Clock. This gave Tommy a few more seconds to try to spear the nest with his makeshift rescue kit. He reached into the great cogs once again and this time pierced the nest and was able to pry it from its dangerous place and put it to rest in the rafters above the clocks working parts in a place of safety. Meanwhile Henry Hardhat was left hanging from the Hour Hand until Tommy reached out to him from inside the Tower and pulled him inside to safety.

At that moment the cogs and wheels all turned noisily together, the Great Bell chimed and the Hatsoff Anthem started to play. You can imagine the noise inside the Tower. Tommy and Henry went quickly down the stairs and into the street. All the locals where there to greet them and to cheer them for their gallant rescue of the birds, the cat and the Fire Chief. Tommy and Henry just stood and looked at all the happy cheering faces. Neither of them could hear a thing after the noise of the Tower so they just smiled and waved to everybody.